Cinderella

Miles KeLLy

Once upon a time, there was a young girl called Cinderella. She lived with her mean stepmother and two stepsisters.

She worked hard all day long and at night she slept by the fireside, in the ashes.

One day, a letter arrived from the palace. The prince was holding a ball, and everyone was invited. Cinderella's stepmother said to her, "You cannot go. You must stay here and mind the fires."

On the day of the ball, Cinderella helped her stepsisters get ready. "Have fun at home!" they teased.

Poor Cinderella watched the carriage drive away, then sat down, almost in tears.

"How I wish I could go to the ball," she said.

Suddenly, a kind-looking old lady appeared! She had glittery wings and a wand. "Hello Cinderella," she said.

"I'm your fairy godmother. I will grant you your wish."

"You shall go to the ball!"

Cinderella's fairy godmother smiled and said, "first we need a way to get you to the palace. Fetch the largest pumpkin from the vegetable patch!"

She waved her wand
and the pumpkin became
a carriage!

"Now you need some horses and a driver to take you to the palace!" said the fairy godmother.

And in two flicks of her wand,
four mice became four horses,
and a rat became a coachman.

"Now for the most important part," said Cinderella's fairy godmother, "your gown."

She twirled her wand, and when Cinderella looked down she was wearing a beautiful dress, and sparkling glass slippers.

Cinderella's fairy godmother said she was ready for the ball, but that she must be home by midnight. "The spell will end as the clock strikes twelve!"

When Cinderella arrived at the palace everyone turned to look at her. "Who is that beautiful young lady?" they asked.

Nobody recognized her, not even her stepsisters.

The prince danced with Cinderella all evening. She was enjoying herself so much that she didn't notice the time.

Suddenly the clock began to strike twelve! Cinderella ran from the palace but in her haste she lost one of her glass slippers!

When Cinderella returned to her carriage the spell had broken. She ran home quickly to make sure she was back before her stepsisters.

The prince, meanwhile, could not forget Cinderella. He had fallen in love and declared that he would marry the owner of the glass slipper.

He visited every house in the land, but had no luck. Finally, he arrived at Cinderella's house.

"This glass slipper belongs to the girl I danced with at the ball," the prince said, "I must find her."

Cinderella's stepsisters invited the prince inside, then they tried to force their big feet into the slipper, but with no luck!

The prince asked if there were any other young ladies at the house. "Of course not," said the stepsisters.

Just then, Cinderella stepped into the room, but before she could speak her stepmother said, "No, not her, she works in the kitchen – she didn't go to the ball."

But the prince asked Cinderella to sit down on the chair. She placed her foot in the glass slipper and it fitted perfectly! Everyone was amazed!

Suddenly, the prince recognized Cinderella as the girl from the ball, and he was overjoyed! "I have found my bride at last," he cried. "Will you marry me?"

Cinderella said yes, and they lived happily ever after.